Littl

A series of hea
stories about a mixed race little
girl called Gemma.

This bright and humorous little
pre-schooler, shares her every
day experiences with other young
children and infants, in the hope
that the adult sharing this story
with them, will discuss any issues,
fears or concerns raised. This will
support the development of the
child's social and emotional
intelligence. Having an opportunity
to discuss fears and anxieties can
reduce stress and encourage
positive mental health and a
sense of well being.

Dedicated to:
my fantastic Nia Bobinski
(Babi),
my awesome Daniel Duck
(BooBoo)
&
my incredible Mary-Louis...E
(Woo).

This book was written for my children before my first child was born.

All of my children love these funny stories and we talk for ages about the issues raised.

I am sure that children everywhere will love these stories too.

Look carefully at each picture.
They are all the same you might say – but look again!

Spot all the differences and send the answers to
browncherub@hotmail.com
with your name, age and address to win a free prize.

Reading is fun!
The illustrations are in black
and white so that your child
can explore their own
creative talents and colour
them in as they wish. Can
they make each picture
different? Then you could
add a picture of your own to
show a happy ending.

Enjoy!

<u>Dinner Wars</u>

When I had my dinner,
just the other day.
I wasn't very happy,
So I had to say...

"Mummy I'm not eating,
any of my dinner!"
"Yes you are,"
she said to me.
"Or you will become thinner."

"No, I won't" I said again,
Clear and long and loud.
I pushed my plate
on to the floor,
And sat there feeling proud.

"I will not eat the carrots!
I will not eat the peas!
Now can I have some
ice- cream?
Can I Mummy, please?"

"No you can't have pudding!
Your dinner's on the floor!
Come and clean
this mess up!
Open the cupboard door!"

"Now take out the dust-pan,
And the little brush."
She made me pick
up everything,
And told me not to rush.

"Now put that food
into the bin,
And give this plate try."
I tried to say
"I'm sorry, Mum,"
But I began to cry.

I cried and cried
into my plate.
I hate veg in my tummy.
"You're going to eat
some of them.
Mum said, "...as veg is
yummy!"

"But why?" I sobbed into my
hands.
"They look like rabbit poo!"
"Oh Gem, they don't,"
she said to me,
"They're really good for you.

"Ok," I said and
closed my eyes.
These peas I had to eat.
I popped them all into
my mouth.
And wriggled in my seat.

"Good girl," Mum said
and kissed my face,
"You really are a winner."
I ate my ice-cream
as I thought…
"Why can't this be dinner?"

Author
Myrah Duckworth
B.Ed Hons

Teacher (1996)
Life coach & mentor

I have been writing books for children and young people for over twelve years. Finally, I feel it's time to share them with the world!

Having worked with children for more than twenty years and raising three children of my own, I know that both the young and old have many concerns and issues that they don't always get an opportunity to discuss. These lovely stories provide that opportunity.

I live in Birmingham with my three beautiful children and my amazing fiancé.

My family and friends are my world. Thanks to you all. Thanks to Teswal and Cheryl for believing in this project. Thanks Tony L. Brown for lighting the way. Thanks to The Most High for blessing me with this creative talent.

<u>Illustrator</u>
Mayuko Taniguchi

Self taught artist & illustrator
Mayuko lives in Japan with her gorgeous son and loving husband.

Proof-reader
Annika Rowbury-Harrison

Teacher of languages

Recommendations
Chris & Rachel Hemming
Just The Two Of Us Child-Minding

And then the eating one was very accepting if the child's feelings in a 'no nonsense' kind of way....again, loads of avenues to explore healthy eating etc.

Steven Brown B.Phil.
Community, Youth and Play Work

With over 20 years of formal and informal education with toddlers, children, young people, adults, parents and families, Little Gem's are so refreshing and inclusive. Written with grace, sensitivity and understanding of the target audience and need for explanation of taboo subjects, such as step families, mixed ethnicity and other things children often question. I can already see the animated version; these stories really are little Gems.

Toni-Anne Butterworth-Myers B.SC, M.SC, Family Worker, Trainee Occupational Psychologist

I have worked with various parents around parenting for connecting emotionally and socially with their children and part of this has included emphasising the importance of reading to their children as a form of bonding. The Little Gems books in particular really offer the parents the opportunity to step into the world of children since
Gem speaks so openly, honestly and innocently about real-life childhood experiences which can be considered to be of a sensitive nature. They address much needed family issues which need to be

spoken about in schools and families and also represent the current family settings. I thoroughly enjoyed the collection and am pleased to share them all with my own child.

Other titles in the Little Gem's series include:
Mummy's Lost
Where Is Teddy?
He Took My Book
I'm Not Scared
... and many others.

Sponsored by my favourite lovely lady in the whole world. Thank you so much for believing in me. Without you, none of this would have been possible.

Printed in Great Britain
by Amazon

46074057R10016